A
ROMAN
SOLDIER

Series Editor:
Giovanni Caselli

Story Consultant:
Joe Loh

Illustrations:
Sergio

Book Editor:
Claire Llewellyn

Series Design:
Caselli Associates

Production:
Susan Mead/Marguerite Fenn

This edition published in 1992 by
Peter Bedrick Books
2112 Broadway
New York, NY 10023

Published by agreement with Simon & Schuster Young Books
Simon & Schuster Ltd, Hemel Hempstead, England

Library of Congress Cataloging-in-Publication Data
Caselli, Giovanni, 1939–
A Roman soldier.

(Everyday life series)
Bibliography: p.
Summary: Presents the story of a young auxiliary
soldier at a fortress on Hadrian's Wall, depicting life in
the Roman Army in the third century A.D.
1. Rome. Army – Juvenile literature. 2. Soldiers –
Rome – Juvenile literature. [1. Rome. Army.
2. Soldiers – Rome] I. Title. II. Series: Caselli,
Giovanni, 1939– . Everyday life of.
DG 89.C37 1986 355′.00937 86-4366

ISBN 0-87226-106-9

Printed and bound by
Henri Proost, Turnhout, Belgium
5 4 3 2

A ROMAN SOLDIER

PETER BEDRICK BOOKS
NEW YORK

Contents

Introduction

This book tells the story of Marcus, a young Roman soldier, who lived around AD 250. He was born in a district called Germania Inferior, which is now part of modern Belgium. When he was about 18 years old, Marcus left his home village to join the Roman army. He became a soldier in the First Cohort (a group of 1000 men) of the Tungrian Regiment. Not long after he joined them, they were sent to guard the fortress of Vercovicium (now known as Housesteads) on Hadrian's Wall in the north of England.

There were two main types of soldier in the Roman army, auxiliaries and legionaries. Auxiliaries, like Marcus, were recruited to defend the well-established frontiers of the Roman Empire from attack by outsiders. Legionaries were sent to conquer new lands for the Empire, or else to guard particularly wild and dangerous frontiers. Like all auxiliaries, Marcus promised to serve with the army for 25 years.

The fortress of Vercovicium was built around AD 150. It was destroyed by raiders in AD 197 and rebuilt a few years later. The Tungrian Regiment was first sent to guard it in AD 211. While they were on duty, it was attacked many times by tribesmen from the North. It was finally abandoned around AD 400, when the Romans withdrew from Britain.

We know a lot about the lives of Roman soldiers because archaeologists have excavated several of the Roman forts along Hadrian's Wall. Roman historians also wrote about the army and its famous battles and campaigns.

At the end of this book you can see a reconstruction of the fort Marcus would have lived in, and some of the objects he would have used in his daily life. There are also suggestions for books to read.

Joining the Army

'By the gods, it's cold!' Marcus shivered, blowing on his hands to warm them. He was taking the last daylight watch, and night was approaching. He stared at the bleak moorland all around.

'I must have been mad to join up. I should never have listened to that merchant!' Marcus thought back to that fateful day in his home village, six months ago. Marcus and his brothers had brought vegetables from their little farm to sell at the market. Business had been slow, and they had gone into the inn for a warming drink.

'It's hardly worth growing the things for this price,' Marcus had grumbled, counting the few coins they had earned. 'How can a man expect to get on in the world?'

A travelling merchant had overheard him. 'How old are you, lad?' he had asked Marcus.

'Eighteen next month. Why do you ask?'

'Well, why don't you join the army?' the merchant had said. 'It's not bad pay, free bed and board for 25 years, and Roman citizenship at the end of it. It's the best way to see the world.'

'Well, I'd quite like to see the world,' Marcus had answered him. 'At least, I'd like to see a bit more of it than our vegetable garden! But me, a soldier? No!' He shook his head.

All the same, he had thought about the merchant's words all the way home. Their family farm was small, and he saw a lifetime of hard work and low wages stretching ahead of him.

So, on New Year's Day, he had sworn the Military Oath, along with a hundred or so other new recruits. Now he was an auxiliary soldier in the First Cohort of Tungrians. His wish to travel had soon been granted. The Tungrians had been sent to the fort of Vercovicium on the great stone wall built on the orders of Emperor Hadrian in northern Britain. The wall kept out the wild Caledonian tribes who lived beyond.

There were no tribesmen to be seen now. Marcus roused himself from his thoughts of the past. The winter sun was setting and the bitter northern night closing in fast. He was glad that guard duty would soon be over.

Life inside the Fort

A squad of soldiers arrived to take over guard duty, and Marcus and his comrades marched briskly back to the fort.

It was dark by now. Marcus could see the welcoming lights of the vicus twinkling ahead. They marched past the bathhouse and came to the main gate in the east wall of the fort.

'I hope Tullius isn't on duty,' whispered Marcus's friend Julius. 'He always takes forever to check our names.'

They were out of luck. Carefully and very slowly the man on sentry duty crossed their names off on his list of men who had been given permission to leave the fort. At last they were allowed out, and hurried to the barracks where they lived with the rest of their troop.

It had taken Marcus some time to get used to all the names of the different units within the army. There were about 80 men in his troop, which was called a century. There were 12 centuries altogether in the First Cohort of the Regiment, which had been sent to guard the fort. So in all there were nearly 1000 soldiers there.

Julius sniffed the air. 'Mutton stew again for supper,' he said.

'I don't care,' Marcus replied. 'I'm starving.'

After they had eaten, Marcus and Julius went back to the room they shared with six other soldiers. Their mate Septimus looked up from the game of dice that was being played. He was winning! 'Do you fancy a bet, Marcus?' he asked.

'No thanks, I'm tired.' Marcus yawned. 'I'm going to bed. But I'd better see what I'm meant to be doing tomorrow first.' He checked the duty roster that hung on the wall of their room. Each soldier's duties were listed on it day by day.

'Sentry duty at headquarters and then a free afternoon. Good! I can go to the vicus and buy a pair of boots.' Marcus turned to Julius. 'It says here that you have tomorrow afternoon free as well. Shall I meet you in the inn?'

'Yes!' grinned Julius. 'You owe me a drink!'

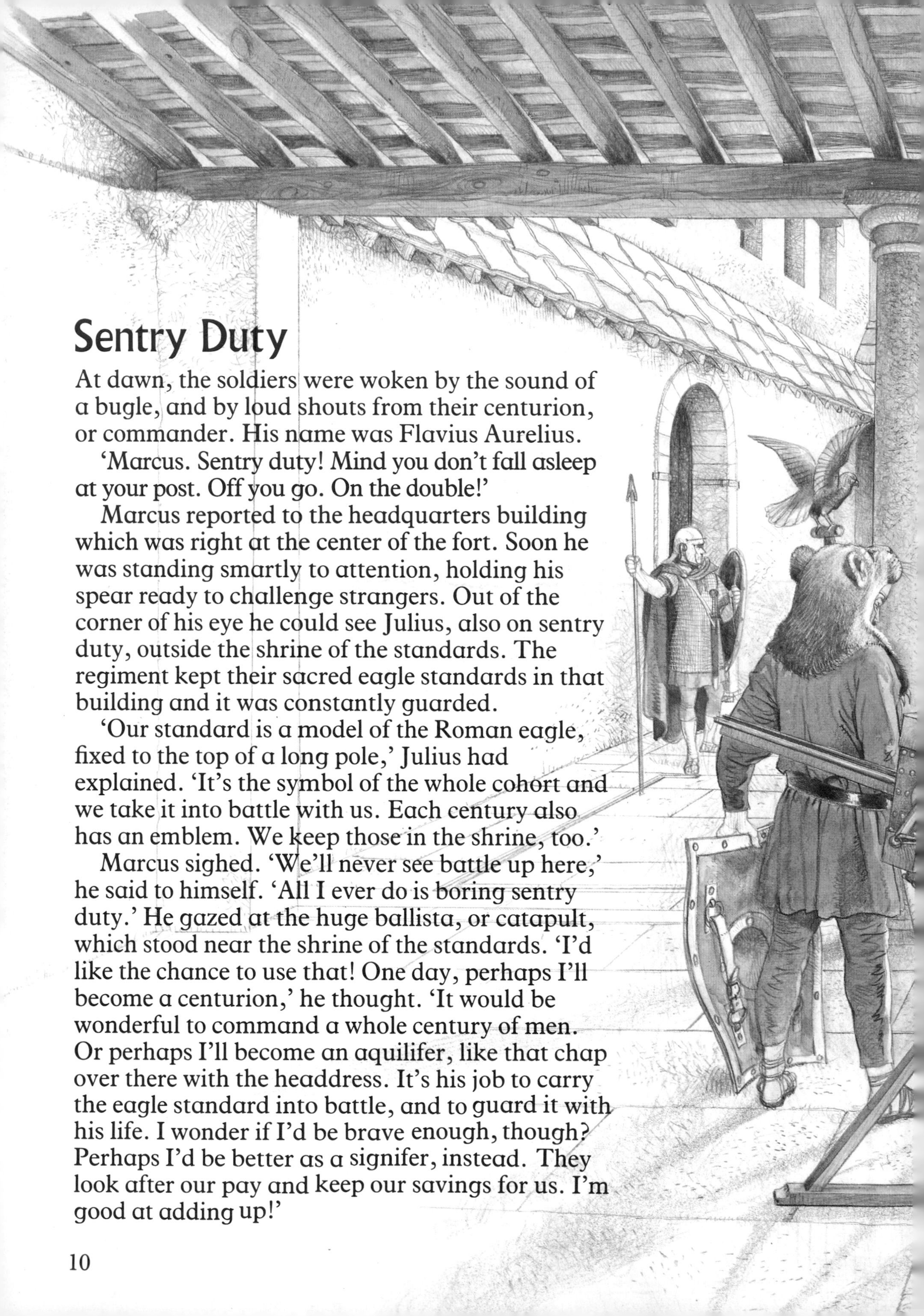

Sentry Duty

At dawn, the soldiers were woken by the sound of a bugle, and by loud shouts from their centurion, or commander. His name was Flavius Aurelius.

'Marcus. Sentry duty! Mind you don't fall asleep at your post. Off you go. On the double!'

Marcus reported to the headquarters building which was right at the center of the fort. Soon he was standing smartly to attention, holding his spear ready to challenge strangers. Out of the corner of his eye he could see Julius, also on sentry duty, outside the shrine of the standards. The regiment kept their sacred eagle standards in that building and it was constantly guarded.

'Our standard is a model of the Roman eagle, fixed to the top of a long pole,' Julius had explained. 'It's the symbol of the whole cohort and we take it into battle with us. Each century also has an emblem. We keep those in the shrine, too.'

Marcus sighed. 'We'll never see battle up here,' he said to himself. 'All I ever do is boring sentry duty.' He gazed at the huge ballista, or catapult, which stood near the shrine of the standards. 'I'd like the chance to use that! One day, perhaps I'll become a centurion,' he thought. 'It would be wonderful to command a whole century of men. Or perhaps I'll become an aquilifer, like that chap over there with the headdress. It's his job to carry the eagle standard into battle, and to guard it with his life. I wonder if I'd be brave enough, though? Perhaps I'd be better as a signifer, instead. They look after our pay and keep our savings for us. I'm good at adding up!'

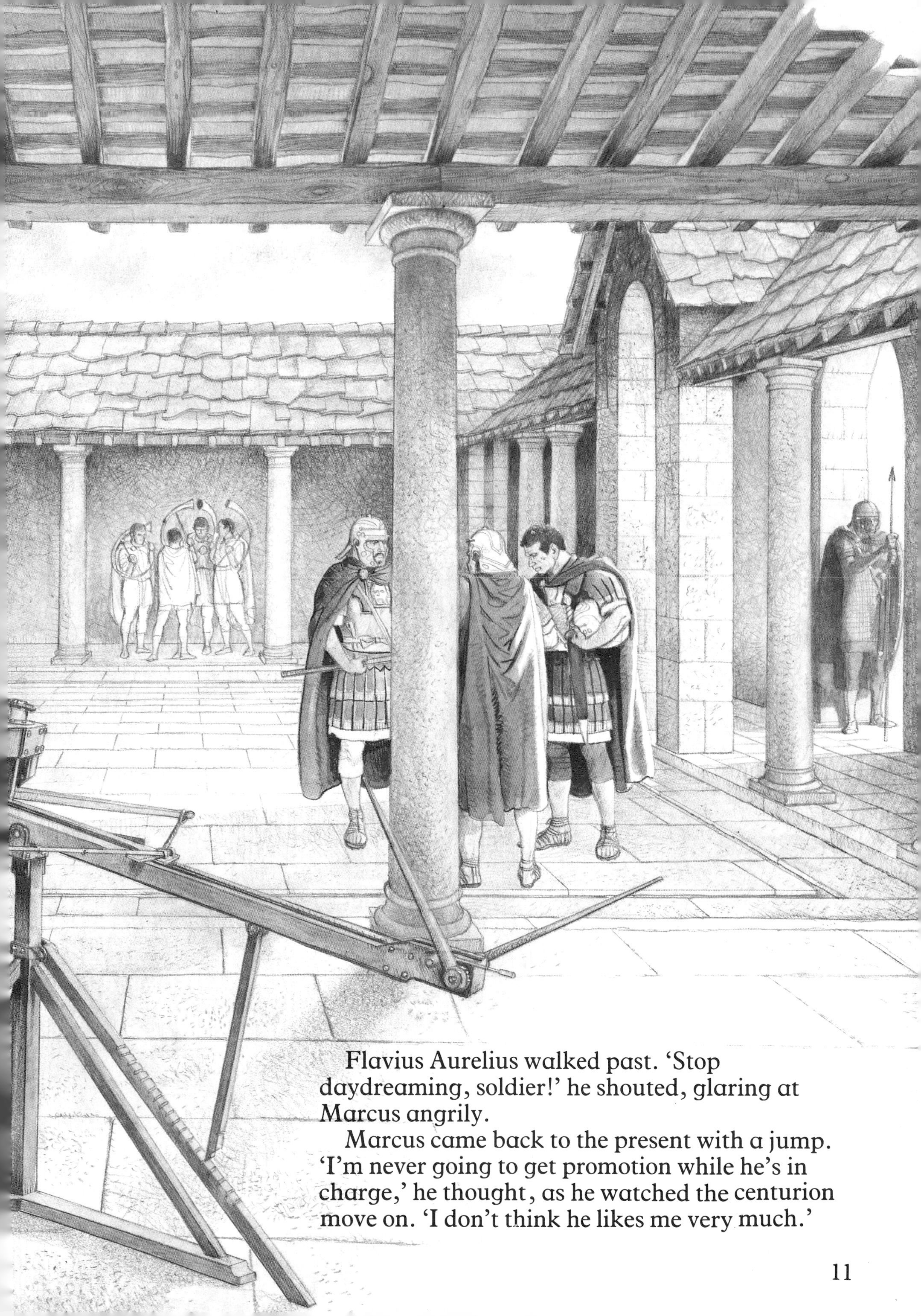

Flavius Aurelius walked past. 'Stop daydreaming, soldier!' he shouted, glaring at Marcus angrily.

Marcus came back to the present with a jump. 'I'm never going to get promotion while he's in charge,' he thought, as he watched the centurion move on. 'I don't think he likes me very much.'

The New Boots

Marcus walked along the main street of the fort. He gave his name to the sentry on duty at the gate, and stepped outside. The untidy streets of the vicus, where the civilians lived, stretched in front of him. There were twice as many civilians as soldiers at Vercovicium. There were craftsmen, merchants, entertainers, and innkeepers. Many soldiers had wives and children living in the vicus, even though this was against the army's rules.

Marcus made his way through the crowded marketplace, towards the shoemaker's shop. The vicus was always noisy. Heavy ox-carts rumbled over the cobbled streets, and children shouted as they chased each other through the narrow alleyways between the houses.

The shoemaker sat outside his house. 'Can I help you, soldier?' he asked.

'I need some good strong boots,' said Marcus.

'Well, I can make you some to order, but that will take time.' The shoemaker looked at Marcus's feet. 'But I think I might have a ready-made pair that would fit.' He rummaged at the back of his workshop. 'Now, try these on for size. They were made for Flavius Aurelius, but he doesn't want them now. If they fit, you can have them cheap.'

Marcus smiled to himself as he tried the boots on. They fitted well enough. He got out his money. 'I'll take them,' he grinned. He walked out of the workshop wearing the new boots and made his way to the inn. He could hear Julius's laugh. He couldn't wait to tell him that he was wearing their centurion's boots.

Weapons Practice

The next day, Marcus and his friends had weapons training in the morning. During his first few months in the army, there had been training every day, and sometimes twice a day. There had been endless drills, long route marches carrying full packs and weapons, and practice in camp-building. Marcus had also been taught to swim. He had already known how to ride, but other soldiers who did not know received instruction.

Now they did not have training sessions so frequently. There had been no fighting in Britain for years, or so Marcus had been told.

'So what's the use of all this?' grumbled Julius, as they made their way to the practice ground. The soldiers all wore their chain-mail armor, and carried their weapons – a short sword, a spear and an oval shield.

'Right, men!' shouted Flavius Aurelius. 'Use those wooden stakes as dummies for sword fighting and show me what you can do!'

Marcus and his comrades practiced lunges and sword thrusts until they were sweating.

'Stop!' yelled Flavius Aurelius. 'Let's see if you can do any better in hand-to-hand fighting. That's what you'll need to be good at to survive in a real fight, you know. Keep the tips of your swords covered all the time. We don't want any nasty accidents!'

Marcus and Julius practiced together. They ducked and dodged each other, swords flashing and jabbing in the pale morning sun. Their centurion called again. 'Good! Now spear-throwing! Aim straight at the enemy's shield. Your turn, Marcus!'

Marcus threw his spear with all his might. It sailed through the air, right over the target shield, and thudded into the earth beyond it.

'Forgotten how to throw, soldier?' Flavius's voice made Marcus cringe. 'You're chucking that spear like a barbarian.'

'But, Sir–' began Marcus.

'Don't argue! A Roman soldier never questions his officers. Extra duties for you this afternoon! Clean out the latrines. I want to see them shine.'

Punished!

Marcus walked gloomily down to the latrine block which stood in the southeast corner of the fort. Inside the latrine building, some men were chatting. Marcus could hear their voices above the noise of the stream which flowed through the building, under the rows of wooden seats. Septimus was there, playing dice, as usual. He laughed when he saw Marcus. 'Latrine duty again?' he said.

Marcus frowned at him. He filled his bucket with water and got down on his hands and knees to scrub the floor.

'Flavius Aurelius must have something against me,' he thought, as he cleaned the floor. 'I was on latrine duty last week as well. The floors and seats are quite easy to clean, but it's so hard to get rid of all the graffiti on the walls.'

Flavius Aurelius marched in to inspect Marcus's work. 'You smell!' he said. 'Report to the bath house.'

Marcus plodded across to the bath house. It stood just outside the fort, near the stream. It had been built some distance away from the other buildings because its furnace, which heated the water, was a fire risk. The baths were used by soldiers and by people from the vicus. Everyone enjoyed the luxury of a soak in the hot water.

Julius stood in the changing room, rubbing oil into his skin to get the dirt off. 'Phew!' he said. 'Don't come too close!'

Marcus also rubbed his skin with oil, and followed Julius into the hot room. Steam billowed all around them. Marcus scraped the dirty oil from his skin, then went through into the next room and plunged into the bath of hot water. That felt better! He was clean at last!

Dangerous Journey

Marcus and the others were playing dice in their room. Suddenly the centurion burst in.

'We have to collect supplies from Corstopitum tomorrow, to deliver to Habitancum,' he told them. 'Since you lot seem to have nothing better to do than play dice, I've put your names down as volunteers to be the escort. We leave at sunrise.'

'Where's Corstopitum?' asked Marcus, when Flavius Aurelius had gone.

Septimus knew. 'About 48 kilometers south.'

'And the other place, Habitancus?'

'Oh, that's north of the wall,' Septimus replied. The whole journey will take us about six days.'

Marcus did not like the idea of six days in the company of Flavius Aurelius. Still, it would be an adventure. Who knew what lay north of the wall?

They woke early the next day. Marcus and Septimus harnessed the oxen to the heavy four-wheeled wagon, and loaded it with leather tents, food for the journey and, of course, their weapons. They set off on foot, with Septimus leading the oxen. The centurion rode on horseback at the rear of their procession. The cart rumbled its way through the vicus, which was unusually quiet at this hour of the morning. They made their way south, along the causeway across the moors. It was a cold grey morning, but Marcus was excited at the prospect of an adventure. At last he was doing something other than sentry duty!

Later that day, they reached the Stanegate Road. Flavius Aurelius gazed at it with pride.

'Beautiful straight road, that,' he said. 'Built years ago when we first conquered this province. Roads like that made our Empire. Good supply lines. The only way to run an efficient army!'

At the Inn

It was dusk when they arrived at Corstopitum. Flavius Aurelius took them to the mansio, the inn for travellers on official or army business. He ordered rooms for the night. Septimus stabled and fed the oxen, and then joined Marcus and the other soldiers. They had an excellent meal.

'You can go for a drink if you like, lads,' said the centurion kindly, 'but don't stay late. We've got another early start in the morning.'

The soldiers hurried off to the inn before Flavius Aurelius could change his mind.

'He's like a different man!' exclaimed Marcus. 'It must be the air, or perhaps he's pleased to get out of the fort, too.'

They found a table to sit at, near the fireplace. A dark, lean soldier sat at the next table. He looked up when they arrived.

'Will you drink with me, friends?' he asked.

'Why not? Come and join us,' replied Julius.

The soldier moved across to their table.

'I'm a Hamian archer, from Syria,' he said. 'We're garrisoned near by. I've come to collect some new bows from the military stores. What about you?'

'We're collecting grain to take to Habitancum,' replied Septimus.

'North of the wall, eh?' said the Syrian. 'Be on your guard. I hear that the Selgovae tribes up there are getting restless.'

'Perhaps we'll see some action at last!' thought Marcus.

Early next morning, they loaded the heavy ox-cart with grain from Corstopitum's granaries. The town was busy, despite the early hour. Craftsmen were hammering out tools and weapons in their workshops. Masons were building new storehouses. Civilians and laden mule-carts jostled in the streets. When the last sack was full of grain, the soldiers set off. They marched north along Dere Street. At noon they reached the great wall, and passed through the Port Gate. Now they were beyond the frontier.

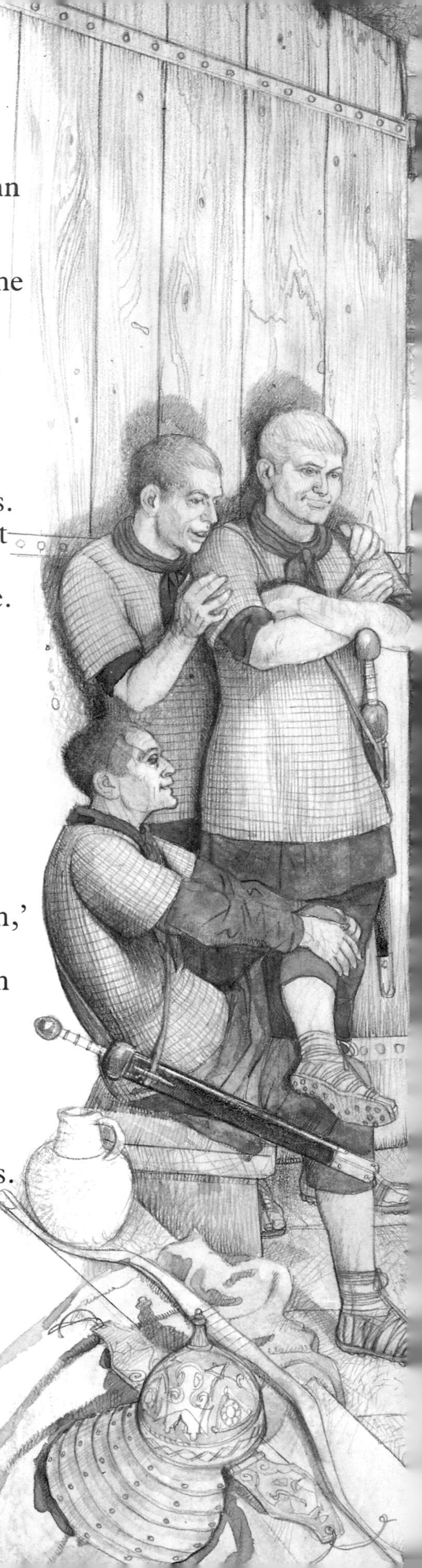

Ambush!

The journey north took two days. At the end of the first day, they pitched their tents on the site of an old marching camp. Flavius Aurelius explained that this was a relic from the days when the army had been campaigning in Caledonia, and trying to conquer the whole country. Now the campaigns had stopped and the wall formed the border.

They took turns at guard duty throughout the night, but nothing happened.

'Suspiciously quiet,' said Flavius Aurelius.

They reached Habitancum by nightfall on the second day. They unloaded the grain and stayed overnight in the army barracks. Next morning, they set off for home. The country seemed deserted.

Marcus was disappointed that nothing exciting had happened to them. He looked at the road stretching ahead through wooded hills. 'What a perfect place for an ambush,' he thought to himself. Suddenly he caught sight of a man running through the trees, and a band of wild-looking men waving swords and axes came hurtling down the slope.

'Selgovae!' yelled Flavius Aurelius. 'Attack!'

Marcus and his comrades drew their swords and raised their shields. Within seconds the tribesmen had reached them. Flavius Aurelius charged into their midst, his spear thrusting and stabbing with deadly skill. Marcus managed to put one man out of action, but slipped and a tribesman's axe slammed down against his shield. Marcus thought his end had come, but Julius slashed at the tribesman with his sword, and the powerful Selgovae fell to the ground.

Julius and Marcus rushed back into the battle, but the tribesmen – dismayed at the soldiers' skill – soon turned and fled.

The Old Man

Flavius Aurelius sent Marcus to see the fort's doctor as soon as they got back to Vercovicium. The doctor, a Greek, examined the gash on Marcus's shield arm.

'You'll live,' he said kindly, 'but stick to light duties only for the next week or so.'

Marcus reported back to the centurion. He half expected him to be angry that he could not play his full part in the life of the fort. But Flavius Aurelius was proud of his soldiers.

'You did well in that ambush. I'll make soldiers of you yet,' he said.

He sent Marcus to act as sentry on one of the gates that was hardly ever used. 'Not much to do there,' he said.

Marcus stood in the gateway. His arm hurt a little, but he didn't feel too bad. At last he had seen some action! Slowly, he became aware of footsteps approaching over the cobblestones. An old man came trudging up the steep path to the gate, leading a mule laden with baskets. Marcus stopped him at the gate.

'What have you got there?' he asked.

'Just fish,' said the old man. 'Some trout for the shop in the vicus.'

The old man looked at Marcus's arm. 'That's a nasty injury you've got there,' he said.

'We were ambushed,' replied Marcus, proudly. 'A Selgovae barbarian did that to me.'

'Barbarian, was he?' murmured the old man thoughtfully.

Marcus suddenly realized that the old man was a Selgovae tribesman himself.

'We are not barbarians,' said the old man gently. 'We just want to be left in peace. We are frightened that you will try to take our lands away from us again.'

He walked slowly through the gate, towards the vicus. Marcus watched him go.

The Temple of Mithras

Guard duty at the gate was over. Marcus hurried back to the barracks. He put his sword and shield away in the equipment room, and picked up a thick hooded cloak which he pulled over his shoulders. It was growing dark as he stepped quickly out through the south gate of the fort. He soon found the path that wound down the hillside between the terraced fields. Scrambling down, he reached the little footbridge at the bottom of the valley. He crossed it, and stood in front of the doorway of the temple of Mithras.

The soldiers at the fort worshipped many different gods. Septimus had sworn loyalty to Jupiter. Others preferred Mars or Hercules or their other local gods. But Marcus, and most of his friends, thought that Mithras, the god of light, was the proper god for a soldier to worship. They believed that soldiers who were faithful to Mithras and fought evil in this world would be rewarded with a place in heaven when they died.

Marcus knocked at the temple door. It was opened by a priest. Marcus entered silently. The temple was like a cave inside. The only light came from two torches on either side of the entrance. Gradually Marcus's eyes got used to the dark, and he could see about a dozen soldiers there. One of them was Flavius Aurelius. He was a full brother in the fellowship of Mithras. You had to pass seven tests of skill and courage before you could become a full brother. Marcus had only just passed the first test which allowed him to join the brotherhood.

Marcus put on the raven-head mask that the brothers wore, and sat down to pray. He looked at the carved picture above the altar. It showed Mithras sacrificing the bull of evil. Now that he had taken part in a real battle, Marcus felt that at long last he was a proper soldier. The merchant had been right; it was the life for him. From now on, he vowed, he would try to fight evil and the enemies of Rome, following the teachings of Mithras – and Flavius's good example.

Picture Glossary

Hadrian's Wall was built between AD 120 and 130. It was 4.5 meters high and 3 meters thick, and very well defended with turrets, mile-castles and forts (such as Housesteads Fort below). The wall formed the border between northern and southern Britain, and was guarded by soldiers from the time it was built until AD 410.

It was also the soldiers' task to protect the traffic on the road from Carlisle to Corbridge (see the map opposite).

Right: This map shows the Roman Empire during the reign of the Emperor Hadrian, who died in AD 138. Hadrian's Wall marked the northern frontier of the Empire.

Housesteads Fort
A Workshop
B Hospital
C Granary
D Headquarters
E Commandant's house
F The village (vicus)

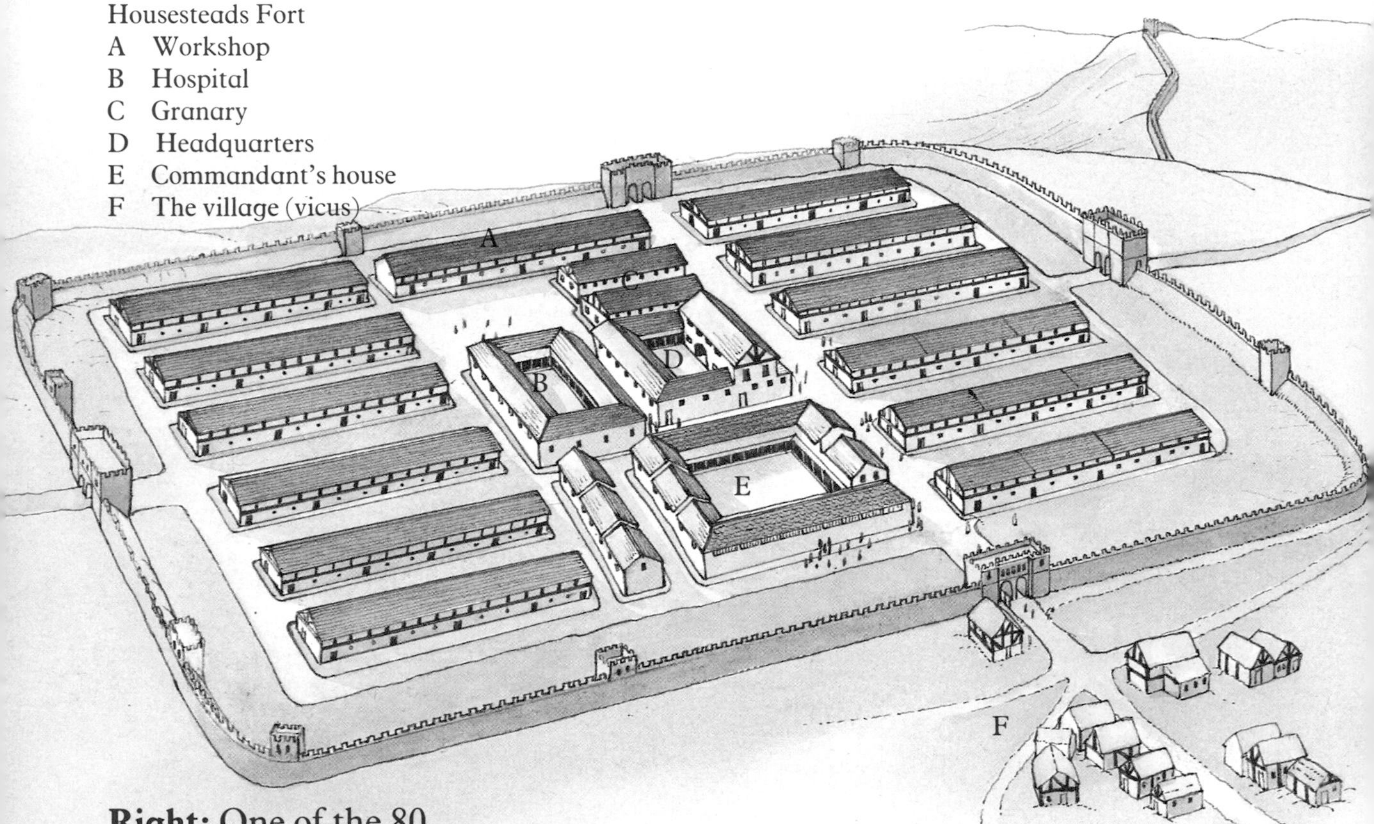

Right: One of the 80 mile-castles (built a Roman mile apart) that defended the wall. The castle is protected by an earth bank, then a fighting ditch, and then another bank, called the vallum.

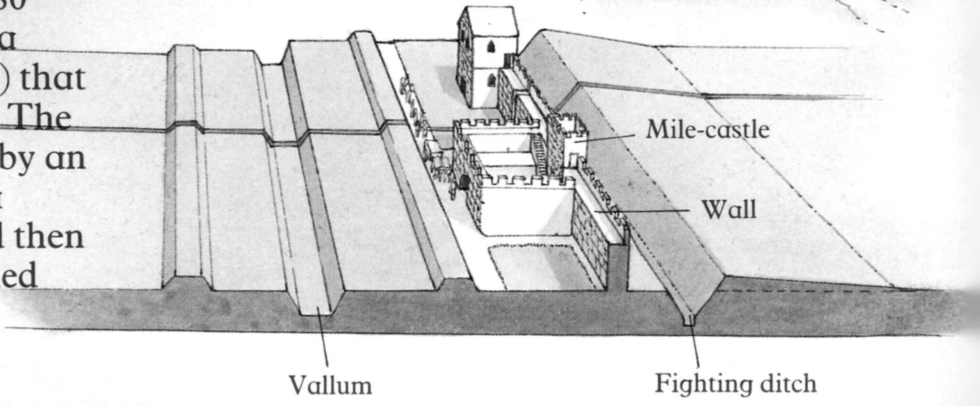

Mile-castle
Wall
Vallum
Fighting ditch

Hadrian's Wall stretched from Carlisle in the West to Wallsend, near Newcastle, in the East. The names of the forts and towns along the wall are shown below.

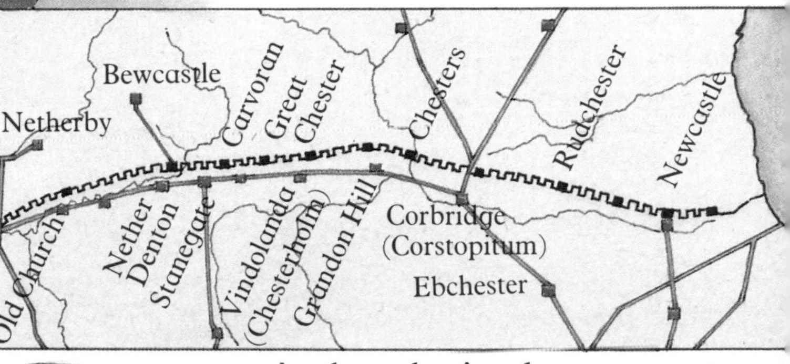

Archaeologists have found many objects used by the soldiers and their families in their everyday lives. These objects (left and below) were found near Hadrian's Wall.

1 Portable altar
2 Altar to Mithras
3 Coin showing Hadrian
4 Wooden comb
5 Pots and a bowl
6 Oil lamp
7 Women's brooches
8 Gold ring
9 Bone hairpins
10 Earring
11 Bronze amulet
12 Men's brooches
13 Board game
14 Tacks on the sole of a sandal
15 Soldier's sandal
16 Reconstruction of sandal

Finding Out More

Books to Read

The following books contain information about life in the Roman Army:

G. Caselli **The Roman Empire and the Dark Ages** (History of Everyday Things series) Peter Bedrick Books 1985
J. Rutland **A Roman Town** (See Inside series) Warwick 1977
M. Corbishley **What Do We Know About the Romans?** Peter Bedrick Books 1992
M. Corbishley **The Roman World** Warwick Press 1986
P. Connolly **Tiberius Claudius Maximus: The Cavalryman** (Rebuilding the Past series) Oxford University Press 1989
K. Usher **Heroes, Gods & Emperors from Roman Mythology** (The World Mythology series) Peter Bedrick Books 1992

You may need an adult to help you read the following books, but they contain a lot of fascinating information:

A. Birley **The People of Roman Britain** U. of California Press 1980
D. Breeze **The Northwest Frontiers of Roman Britain** St. Martin's Press 1982
R. Ling **The Roman World** (Making of the Past series) Peter Bedrick Books 1988
S. Perowne **Roman Mythology** (Library of the World's Myths and Legends) Peter Bedrick Books 1983